THE GATES OF HELL

THE RIVERS OF HELL 0.5

LIANA VALERIAN

Cover art and design by Shaunie Anne Schoonejans.

CIP - Kataložni zapis o publikaciji
Narodna in univerzitetna knjižnica, Ljubljana
821.163.6-312.9
821.111-312.9
VALERIAN, Liana
The gates of hell : the rivers of hell 0.5 / Liana Valerian. - Brežice :
self-published L. Valerian, 2024. - (The Rivers of Hell ; 0.5)
ISBN 978-961-07-2424-7
COBISS.SI-ID 215663363

*To those who see beyond the darkness to find
the light within.*

CONTENT INFORMATION

Neph and Syrin's story might be the sweetest one in *The Rivers of Hell*. Still, for your safety, I would urge you to read the trigger warnings on my website www.lianavalerian.com.

CONTENTS

GLOSSARY

Archdemon: Strongest and oldest of the demons. The original Fallen who embraced sin.

Ashtaroth: An archdemon known for his wisdom and command over legions.

Asmodai: A powerful archdemon, often associated with lust and wrath.

Azeal: A demon known for his cunning and deceit.

Belial: An archdemon representing corruption and lawlessness.

Elysium: Heaven/Paradise. A realm of peace and beauty, reserved for those who lived noble lives.

The Fallen: Angels who have fallen from grace and are denied re-entry to Heaven for all eternity.

Incubi: Plural of incubus. Sex demons.

The Lethe: The River of Forgetfulness. To drink from it is to lose all memories of one's past.

Malaphar: A demon notorious for his trickery and malice.

Nephithar/Neph: A demon created by Sataniel, calls him Father.

The Phlegethon: The River of Fire

Sataniel: Satan, the ruler of Hell.

Succubi: Plural of succubus. Sex demons.

Syriniana/Syrin: Female angel, an archivist.

Uriel: An archangel associated with wisdom, light, and guidance.

PRONUNCIATION

Syrin: SIGH-rin

Nephithar: NEF-e-thar

Azeal: AH-zeel

Uriel: YOO-ree-el

Asmodai: AZ-mo-dye

Ashtaroth: ASH-ta-roth

Belial: BEE-lee-al

Malaphar: MAH-la-far

SUMERIAN

Muluskara – Shining Moon

Kuguillur – Silver Lilac

Gilsa – Treasure

Emeğir – Native Tongue

Šumer (Akk.) – Land of the Noble Ones

PLAYLIST

Nightwish – *Planet Hell*
Lacrimosa – *Feuer*
Nightwish – *Procession*
Thirty Seconds to Mars – *Stranger in a Strange Land*
Celldweller – *Frozen*
Muse – *Map of the Problematique*
Eurielle – *Forbidden*
Nightwish – *The Siren*
Elley Duhé – *Middle of the Night*
Tristania – *December Elegy*
Within Temptation – *Our Solemn Hour*
Muse – *Compliance*
Evanescence – *The End of a Dream (Synthesis)*
Nine Inch Nails – *The Great Below*
Evanescence – *Lost in Paradise (Synthesis)*
Nightwish – *Gethsemane*
Nightwish – *Feel For You*
Nightwish – *Ghost Love Score (Once)*
Imany – *Don't Be So Shy*
Natasha Blume – *Black Sea*
Ruelle – *War of Hearts*

THE GATES OF HELL

MAP

CHAPTER 1

HELL – THOUSANDS OF YEARS AGO

I grew tired of this battle centuries ago. Ever since we began fighting in mortal forms, the skirmishes have all blended into one – river rapids of gore and carnage. After clashes such as this one, I tend to sit in my study and admire my collection of angel feathers. I must admit, the habit no longer brings the joy it once did. The repetitiveness has numbed me to the simple pleasures of life in Hell.

I slice into the neck of my opponent with a backhanded blow, then crouch to gather one of the feathers the warrior from Heaven shed during our violent collision in the field of battle. Admiring the blue sheen of the barbs, I tuck it into the pouch I carry specifically for this purpose. Angelic feathers, unlike those of Fallen, are all an iridescent variation of white. Their subtleties may be lost on most, but I have a keen eye for them.

Once I straighten, I see that the wounded angel has fled from our confrontation. No matter. Will sending another angel back to their Maker make a difference? It will not.

I, Nephithar, the son of Sataniel, have rightly earned the moniker of Angelbane through my glorious deeds on the warfront. Few angels survive an encounter with my blade, and none leave unscathed.

I should not, however, allow my pastime to dominate so much of my attention in this war between Heaven and Hell, but as it happens, Father created me to be the polar opposite of his mortal form. Where he has silver hair, I have hair of midnight. Where his eyes are the palest of gray, mine are the darkest of red. Where he has wings, I... do not.

Some have dared to insinuate that my fixation on the feathery appendages is an undignified form of jealousy. I do not recall their names anymore. They had only seconds of life left after the statement.

Another angel steps into my path – he must be as tired of these battles as I am if he is facing *me* today. I grip my weapon tightly and sneer at him. The angel holds a golden pike, taller than we are, and his armor reflects the orange sky and scattered lava vents, nearly blinding me with its brilliance.

I lunge at the soldier, my blade hissing as I slice through the air. The angel is quick, though, and parries my strike with the shaft of his pike. The clash of the two weapons rings loudly, even above the cacophony of battle. He pushes against me, spreading his wings and distracting me. Frustrated, I roar as I twist out of the stalemate and slash at him with rapid strikes. The angel, however, deflects each blow with infuriating precision. I have not faced such a worthy opponent in decades.

He thrusts at my heart with all his strength, but I sidestep and slash at a vulnerable point on his side. My blade meets flesh, and the angel stumbles back, losing his footing. Taking advantage of the weakness, I press the attack, my strikes coming faster and harder. His eyes show an awareness of impending defeat, and I laugh triumphantly. With a final, powerful blow, I finish off my quarry. He disappears into the ether before I can collect my tax in feathers, and I grit my teeth. His would have been a great addition.

The screeching of Hell's lower creatures turns my head towards a cliff's edge to the east. Father's newest pets, hellhounds we call them, are ripping the very thing that constantly occupies my thoughts off a downed angel. Wings in tatters, the warrior twitches violently, trying to dislodge the hounds of Hell to no avail. They are vicious creatures.

Demons, Heaven has taken to calling us. Their Fallen angelic brethren, the creations they made, the offspring they begot – to them, it is immaterial. We are all demons. It matters to us, though; we observe a strict hierarchy and in the pecking order of Hell, I am their prince, the heir apparent, their general and commander.

With my chin and sword raised high, I enter the fray again. Slashing, stabbing, kicking, and punching my way through the living and dead flesh in my path, I reach the front ranks and search for another formidable adversary. An archangel perhaps? It has been a while since I crossed swords with Gabriel, that sanctimonious buffoon. Any angel is hard to kill in single combat – unless of course one possesses a strong affinity to manipulate the ether, the very binding of the universe – but killing an archangel... now that would be sung about in all the annals of Celestial history. I am not completely certain I could achieve the feat, but I would gladly fall in an attempt. After all, it is what I was created for, to be the weapon Hell wields against Heaven.

Instead of the brightest of wings, I spot a shimmer of silvery lilac. Drawn to the magnificent feathers, I watch as an angel in the rare female form battles half a dozen of Father's baser creatures. The black-skinned beasts, equipped with claws and fangs, tear into the angel's soft-looking skin. Her hair, silver like Sataniel's, though not nearly as bright, whips around a heart-shaped face as she turns to parry strikes. Her eyes, a perfect blend of the color of her hair and wings, shimmer with pain.

As a snarling demon hooks its claws into the flesh of one of her wings, she pulls it back in reflex, and a shower of delicate feathers envelops the scene, like gentle cherry blossoms in spring winds.

Normally, I would be salivating at the thought of getting my greedy hands on those precious cast-offs. I would already be there, finishing the angel off and shoving fistfuls of the treasure into my pouch. Now, however, all I feel is outrage that such magnificent things could be marred. They are simply spectacular.

"Stop," I growl at the brutish minions as I draw near. The angel glances at me for the briefest of moments, her already large eyes widening further in fear once she sees the Angelbane standing behind her attackers. The demons, however, ignore me, too far gone in bloodlust. "Obey!" I grit through tightly clenched teeth. Nothing.

Their preposterous disobedience enrages me to the point where I fear hellfire will burst out of my nostrils. The barely perceptible creak of my leather gloves against the pommel of my tightly gripped sword is the only warning the demons get before I mow them down, one after another, bathing myself and the angel in their worthless blood.

Still panting in rage, I sheathe my sword and take a step closer to her mangled wing. The angel stumbles back. "I will not hurt you, *Muluskara*." Her brow furrows at the sobriquet, said not in Malachim, but in the Emeğir language of Šumer. No one writes poetry in Hell, but I have seen poets among the talking apes and retained a phrase or two.

Why should she not fear me though? From all she knows, I am the butcher who hacks off the very thing I am staring at now. Silvery drops of blood bead on the feathers of her wing's leading edge. The sight disturbs my refined sensibilities, but also tightens my skin in a way that is not familiar to me. It feels as if my blood is thickening, the sluggish flow of it forcing my heart to beat stronger. Once the suddenly hot blood reaches my pelvis, I can safely attribute a name to these sensations – lust.

In the few hundred years since I have been unleashed upon the world, I have had intercourse numerous times, but I was never the one to initiate it. I only ever truly paid attention to the War. Sex demons, however, have a way of making the body willing. My appearance being as pleasing as it is, they have availed themselves of my mortal form many times, and I have allowed them to do so. As with fighting, I wanted to excel equally at copulation. Failure in any aspect is unacceptable.

Nevertheless, my body is now surely awakening at the sight of bloodied lilac wings, akin to that of a mortal man when faced with his wife's naked breasts for the first time. Is it the high of battle, the lust for blood, or has my obsession taken a new twisted turn?

I reach a slightly trembling hand towards the glistening pearls of blood, wishing I had taken my gloves off. The thought of feeling the wetness of this female's blood on my fingers tightens my groin. The thought of her enjoying my touch, of making her wet elsewhere, makes me moan.

The sound startles both the angel and me. I have never unleashed such a sound before, not while wounded grievously in battle, not even while orgasming when surrounded by a dozen succubi. The angel leaps back and launches herself into the air with a mighty flap of her iridescent wings. Belatedly, I lunge forward, my fingers barely skimming the silk of her robes.

A part of me notes that she is not wearing the gleaming, platinum-colored, angelic plate armor her compatriots are. The majority of my awareness, however, is focused on the fact that I was, once again, distracted by feathers and let my quarry escape. With a few mighty strokes, she disappears into the aerial fray and behind enemy lines.

Clenching my fists, I beat down the urge to throw a tantrum. Lowering my eyes to the ground, I see I stand among shed silvery feathers. I carefully pluck one up by the rachis, making sure not to bend any more barbs as they have already been ruffled in the skirmish. Wishing I could slay the imbecilic demons again, I bring the feather to my nose and inhale deeply. A bouquet of sweet, night-blooming jasmine floods my very being. *The Queen of the Night*. How very fitting, for I would enjoy nothing more than to make her one.

I empty my pouch of the feathers I collected today and make sure to store every last one of hers.

CHAPTER 2

I shoot up in bed and clutch my pulsing member. Semen spills into my palm, then slides down the shaft, joining the rivulets from my stomach to pool together into a sticky mess. Panting, I drop back down, leaning my head back as the last of the spasms wrack my body.

This same scenario has been repeated countless times in the months since encountering the lilac angel on the battlefield. I searched for her, but never saw her again. Considering her attire and prolonged absence from battle, I concluded that she was not a warrior, but a scholar. Why she was there that day, bravely fighting off a number of savage minions, I do not know.

I tried distracting myself with the Daughters of Hell, but it was clear that I had developed another fixation, and substitution just would not work. I would never admit aloud how many times I stroked my own flesh while clutching one of the damned lilac feathers.

As my heartbeat slows, the cooling fluid on my pelvis aggravates me enough that I must take care of it. In my bathing chambers, I wash until no traces of stickiness are left, then use a cloth to pat myself dry. This is incredibly undignified, orgasming in my sleep every time I rest, obsessing over a female – an angel! – whom I've seen only for the briefest of moments. It has to stop now. The time has come to track her down.

After pulling on tight black leathers, I strap on as many knives and short swords as I can. I do not plan on being caught, but I will never go to the heart of the enemy's encampment in Hell unarmed – putting aside the fact that *I should not be going there at all*. This war has lasted for centuries for a reason; we are evenly matched. They outnumber us, but we have the advantage of being on home territory. Heaven will not stop until our royalty agrees to be confined in Hell and to stop interacting with humanity. Tell Hell we cannot do something, however, and we will fight to do the complete opposite. While free will is what we have always fought for, I am about to all but ride into a possible cage merely to assuage the needs of my cock.

I summon my steed and climb onto its bony back, feeling the heat from its infernal core. I then turn the reins toward the Lethe. The

River of Forgetfulness, also flowing through Elysium, is the only area of Hell that could be described as being lush. No wonder the hosts of Heaven decided to use it as a staging ground. I spur my mount into a gallop, its fiery hooves making the only sound in the quiet night.

While there are no moons or suns in Hell, it does follow the daily cycle, the length of the dark and less-dark phases roughly even. The night will not hide noises, however, and I will have to dismount and continue on foot far too soon if I wish to remain unnoticed. Without it, I am far more inconspicuous.

One advantage of having been created by Hell's infamous ruler is that he made me undetectable by both demonic and angelic senses. While they can normally sense each other, with the exception of Celestials strong enough to hide themselves with the ether, I merely become another shadow. That is the plan, at least.

In truth, I am not even completely certain what my goal is tonight. While I am definitely being led to the angel by my manhood, I do not dare dream about her being receptive to my advances. Even if she were not terrified of me, I have never, in all my centuries, had to seduce a female. Or a male, for that matter, but I imagine that task to be far easier. I would not know how to convince her to lie with me, nor do I think I am inclined to force myself onto her. That is another thing I have never done; though I am widely known for my savagery on the battlefield, I find the act of rape to be... unclean, unnecessary, and dishonorable.

As my musings carry me closer to Heaven's outpost, I feel it unsafe to continue mounted. With a slap on its skeletal flank, I dismiss my steed, take stock of my surroundings and plan my trajectory to remain in the shadows as much as possible.

Once the wall the angels built is in sight, I eye the length of it, searching for a possible point of entry. It has been a long time since Hell attacked this outpost directly, and they do not guard it as closely as they could. Since our intelligence points towards an imminent attack, I am hoping the outpost will not be empty. Or at least that my quarry will be there. I refuse to entertain the thought that I may leave here disappointed. I never enter a fight thinking of defeat.

It takes me longer than I would admit to anyone I know to find suitable ingress. Once I enter the encampment, however, I am faced with the task of tracking down my prey.

Over the centuries, the angels transformed this settlement from a temporary one to one of permanence. No tents dot the horizon, and there is no merriment around smoking campfires. Not that angels sully their precious mortal forms with unnecessary organic matter. Nor do they indulge in merriment. No, quiet alleyways between endless rows of identical marble houses – that aligns perfectly with everything I know about the self-righteous, emotionless storks.

Prowling the streets of the angelic war camp, I test the air for any hints of jasmine. Though the scent had mostly faded from her fallen feathers, the fragrance burrowed so deep into my very being that, had I a soul, it would surely smell of her. Her wide inquisitive eyes are all I see when I close mine. My mind had supplied my ever-growing fantasies with the contours of her body, a body whose shape could not be gleaned under those wide silken robes. Something I would not dare to imagine, fearing it would do her no justice, is her voice. I have not heard it. Until this moment.

Inside what must be her wartime home, I hear faint humming, reminiscent of the stringed harps the Kiengir people play. The sound is ethereal, shimmering in the air. The melody, delicate yet haunting, seeps through the air flues like a ghostly whisper, spreading warmth through my chest.

I choke down the urge to scoff, not wanting to give myself away yet. The Butcher of Hell, attempting to describe sounds and melodies to himself – surely the butt of a jest.

The stone and marble walls of her dwelling are overgrown with night-blooming jasmine. The white blooms are open, emanating the scent which clings to her feathers. As I draw closer, my body's reaction to the strong fragrance is instantaneous. My skin feels too tight, stretching thin over muscles that hum just as they do right before a battle. Sparks of warmth bloom over my entire being, as if I were doused by a rain of fire.

23

At that moment, I hear the faintest sounds of metal upon metal – a warrior walking in armor. The increasing volume of the steps, along with a barely perceivable susurration of wings being resettled, tells me that an armed angel is walking in my direction.

Having no choice, I quietly enter my angel's home, making sure the door shuts with the gentlest of snicks.

CHAPTER 3

She sits in a long silken nightdress with her back facing me, still humming, clearly not noticing my sudden presence. Her silver hair is braided and pulled to the front. With it out of the way, I can see, for the first time, the unmarred skin of her back and shoulders. It gleams in the candlelight, shadows dancing over the contours of her shoulder blades as they move with the motions of her arms.

Ignoring my body's reaction to the skin of her arms and nape being on display, I stalk closer, driven by curiosity. What would an angel who is not a warrior be doing in her free time in an army encampment? Once I can see past her shoulders, my brows climb as I discover the answer – she is weaving a basket.

She has already formed the base and built the sides, and is now adding intricate depictions of what look to be date palms. Does she need the basket, or is merely passing the time?

Once my gaze is no longer held by the growing motif, I admire her quick and confident fingers, then, following the movement of bones under her glowing skin, her delicate wrist. When I see the swell of her breasts under the thin material of the sheath she wears, my eyes lock on the sight as if fettered with chains.

I must have made a sound, because the angel stiffens and lifts her head, her nimble fingers now frozen mid-motion. Before she can turn around or raise the alarm, I use an arm atop her sternum to pull her against me and place my other hand over her mouth. She bucks in my hold and her frightened inhale is loud enough that I fear she could call attention to us without even having her mouth free to scream.

"Shh," I whisper in her ear. She immediately stills again. Why? Does she recognize me or is it merely wishful thinking? That she could have perhaps obsessed over me even a third as much as I have over her these past moons... An entire season has passed in the mortals' realm since she last heard my voice, brief as that was.

I lean forward until she can see my face. Once her eyes turn in my direction, her nostrils flare, and, under the hold of my arm, her heart stutters a beat, then resumes a faster tattoo. "I will not hurt you."

Still holding her wide eyes captive, I let my arm slacken and tentatively pull it down, away from her neck. Unfortunately – or perhaps not – the movement allows the side of my hand to slide over one of her breasts, the stiffened peak atop it such a shockingly unexpected change in topography that I inadvertently stop. Once my mind realizes where my hand rests, my cock takes notice as well. Already half stiff since I walked in and saw her bared flesh, it now twitches with need, making me press my pelvis against her lower back in reflex.

Her large silver eyes widen with a different kind of fear and I grit my teeth before forcing myself to put space between any part of her breast and me, as well as any part of her and my cock. "I will not hurt you in *any* way," I reassure her, voicing the intention behind my retreat.

Are those tears gathering at the corners of her eyes? Half of me wishes to leave this instant and throw myself into the ever-blazing inferno of the Burning Pits. But I am unaccustomed to giving up. "Did I not slay the demons attacking you the day we met?" When her expression stays unchanged, I narrow my eyes with impatience. "It takes but one dagger thrown at one tendon to ground an already wounded angel. I did not harm you then and I am not harming you now."

After another quiet moment, she squeezes her eyes shut once in acquiescence. The gesture releases twin silvery tears down her rounded cheeks. As one hits the top of my finger, I carefully withdraw my hand and bring the drop to my lips. I have never tasted tears before. Some of my uncles prefer the kind of sex where tears abound, the pain of their bed partners getting them off more efficiently than the most skilled kneeling succubus, but the only thing that ever got me off was this female's feathers.

Picking the watery bead up with the tip of my tongue, I close my eyes to savor the new sensation, a new part of this angel's body. Salty, yes, but there is also an unexpected hint of sweetness and something almost metallic. The unique combination makes me think of the salted dates Beelzebub once goaded me into eating with hands still bloodied from battle. I much prefer the shimmering manna she produced for me. When I open my eyes, I see that she is staring at me

28

with her mouth half open. Would holding her head still so I can lick the sparkling tracks on her cheeks work counterproductively to the tenuous truce we just established? Probably.

I clear my throat and straighten, inhaling deeply. "I am Nephithar. What are you called, *Kuguillur*?"

One delicately raised silver eyebrow shows me that a measure of incredulity won over her fear. Was it the way I introduced myself, or the new Emeğir moniker?

"I know who you are." Her voice could bring a lesser creature to its knees. Rich and resonant, it fills the small room with an invisible substance.

I raise an eyebrow of my own, wordlessly commanding her to answer my question.

"Why do you wish to know my name, demon?"

The blatant attempt to humble me by throwing me into the same basket as Hell's lower creatures almost makes me want to reply *because I did not know which name to shout while I bring myself to climax with your torn feathers clutched in my fist*, but I resist. In truth, I did not risk sullying her precious feathers like that. Well... I did do it once. I orgasmed so hard my eyes rolled into the back of my head.

The angel must interpret my silence as obstinacy and not sexual fantasies, because she finally answers. "Syriniana. Syrin," she adds, almost as if out of habit. She bites her lower lip, clearly wishing she could take the diminutive back. The fingers of my dominant hand twitch as I fight the urge to release her lip from behind her teeth. I seem to have a strong aversion to her pain in any form.

"Syrin," I nod in greeting, purposefully using the shortened form of her name.

Her lips purse in a slight show of consternation. "What are you doing here, Butcher?"

Her use of the least favorite of my more common sobriquets triggers a sharp sting of... *something*. "Nephithar," I repeat, my voice lower, closer to a growl than I want it to be around this female. I do not wish to frighten her into any unwise actions.

"My home here is too small for me to safely summon my wings. Nephithar." My name said in that mellifluous tone overshadows any pleasure her use of dark humor may have evoked. I allow the sudden weakness in my legs to bring me to my knees next to her still-seated form, my movements slow and purposefully unthreatening. Her jaw all but unhinges at the way I consciously yield the advantageous position.

"Talk to me." Her brows come together in confusion, so I clarify before she can ask what about. "Tell me what you were doing on the battlefield that day."

"I am… an archivist," she replies haltingly. "My assignment is to preserve events in this conflict to the greatest possible detail. I am often present during battles, but that time I was herded into a disadvantageous position."

I glower at her from beneath my brows. "You should not have been close enough to danger to be injured. Why do they let you-?"

She moves faster than even my eyes can track, throwing first one, then another dart, hitting me in the middle of each thigh. I hiss at the sharp sting, my hands going to my daggers by instinct. Before I wrap my fingers over the hilts and possibly ruin any chances of a peaceful conversation, reason returns, and I weigh her actions and our surroundings. An atlatl rests against the wall, explaining why she would be equipped with the small projectiles. She made no mortal threat against me, however, and most importantly, she did not launch the stingers at my manhood, something that would be the perfect target considering my kneeling position.

"I am thousands of years old, demonling," she says once our eyes meet again, the barb straightening my spine. "Just because I do not devote my life to fighting, does not mean I am not more than capable of wielding any weapon in existence. They do not *let me* do anything. It is my right and my purpose."

The fire in her words unclenches my jaw and sends an echo of flame to my mercifully unpunctured groin, stirring the need I have found myself in ever since I first laid eyes on the creature before me.

I pluck the barbs out of my flesh and throw them atop her table. "You are correct, of course. I merely do not wish to see harm come to you."

She scoffs, the sound a melodious tinkle. "Why is that, *Angelbane*? You have no problem murdering my kind in battle."

"That is war and they are soldiers. They do not lose sleep over killing my kind. Or would you have me believe they would not slay an incubus who had never killed anyone, had they come across him in Hell?"

Syrin shakes her head slowly. "Why not simply acquiesce to our demands?"

"And surrender our free will once more?"

"All Heaven wants is to keep the strongest, the archdemons, those who could slay hundreds of mortals in one fell blow, from being able to do so."

I huff incredulously. "You call us that now? Is it not too close to archangel for their liking?"

"We call the original Fallen that," she corrects, and I cannot help but flinch. I am as much royalty as they are. Trembling fingers soft as silk gently tip my chin up until my eyes meet hers. "Why do you care what title Heaven gives you?" she asks, her voice soft and kind. Clearly her good nature overcame any disdain she may feel for me. Were I anyone else, she would have doomed herself by caring. Every hair on my body stands as a wave of horror suffuses me. The need to keep her unmarred is so strong I feel nauseated.

"I do not," I answer, my voice gruffer than I want it to be. I slowly take her hand and turn it so the palm faces me, then rest my cheek on it, gauging her reactions all the while. Her lower lip shakes at the action, but she does not pull her hand out of my gentle hold.

Emboldened, I softly trail my fingers over her wrist, then the smooth skin of her inner arms. Her gaze is locked onto where my hand touches her, and her breaths become panting. "You should not be touching me like that," she protests.

"Have you ever been kissed?" I ask her instead of relinquishing the connection. She rears back in alarm, looking at me once again. "I have not," I admit. I never allowed the demons I experimented with near my face. The sight of her full lips is making me painfully hard, though, and I must have taken leave of my senses attempting to move this fast with an angel.

"You should leave." Her body begins to tremble under my touch. She looks overwhelmed and scared. Frowning with disappointment and impatience, and utterly unwilling to frighten her further, I let my hand drop.

"Forgive me," I whisper. "Will you allow me to stay a while longer?"

She shakes her head, first with drawn brows, as if she is waking from a dream, then more vehemently. "You must leave, demon," she says with force. "If anyone were to see us together, they would think I consort with Hell." I ignore her choice of epithet — I am as much a demon as a lion is a granary cat.

"Then tell them you are merely reforming a heretic." It is instantly obvious that the note of irreverence in my tone is neither lost on her, nor appreciated. Syrin's deep inhale puts her chest in relief, drawing my gaze like an unholy moth to the holy flame. Appreciating my distraction even less than my words, she bristles, reminding me of the quilled creatures roaming Above.

"Do not think so lightly of the position you put me in, Butcher." She gives me a stern look. "That you are still alive does not speak well of me."

I tilt my head. "You would end me, angel?" I do not know whether to be aroused by her confidence or insulted over her estimation of my prowess. Crossing my arms, I lean back and wait for her reply.

"I am still in disbelief that *you* are not here to finish *me*."

My lips stretch into a grin, unused muscles protesting with a twitch in my cheek. "Oh, I would most certainly finish you off, were you to wrestle with me, angel."

Her brows inch together for a second before my meaning becomes clear. I see the precise moment she deciphers the play on words. Her eyes widen, another flush travels up her neck to cover her beautiful face, and her lower lip quivers in dismay before her mouth presses together with evident anger. I press my own lips together tightly as well, attempting to hold my laughter behind them.

Before she can throw any more darts at me, shouting is heard from outside. It is so unlikely for her kind to raise their voices that the possibility of them having caught a hint of my scent cannot be ignored. Syrin's face pales so quickly that, were she a mortal, she would be unconscious on the ground. As it is, her silvery eyes are as round as the mortal's moon. Sighing in resignation, I stand and tip my chin.

"Until tomorrow, *Gilsa*."

She rises with such speed that I unthinkingly extend my arms in readiness to catch her were she to stumble. She merely looks at me with a blank expression. "You will be caught," she says.

I wink at her and, seeing that she is standing securely on her feet, back up towards the exit of her abode. "I am glad you are concerned for my safety, my treasure, but rest assured I will not let them keep us apart."

Without further ado, I slink out of her home and once more blend into the darkness to make my escape.

CHAPTER 4

I leave the angels' outpost without altercations and spend a restless night awake, going over every moment of my encounter with the lilac angel who is even closer to perfection than my dreams and fantasies have led me to believe.

Several times during the day, I have to relieve the aching hardness plaguing me as my head refuses to evict the sound of her voice from the forefront of my thoughts. I count down the hours until I can see her again, almost wishing a battle indeed emerged, just so I can occupy my hands with my sword instead of my abused member.

Finally, night falls, the angels have retired to their homes, and I breach their compound once more. I open the door to my angel's home just wide enough to slide in like a wisp of smoke. Before I can close the door, a dagger thuds against its frame, quivering where it embedded itself into the wood, no more than an inch from my ear. Extending my arm to quietly close us in, I face the object of my obsessions.

She is dressed much in the same way as she was yesterday; a silky sleeveless gown of the purest white. Her hair is unbound today, a waterfall of moonlight cascading around her shoulders. The determined look on her face takes my breath away – she had clearly missed on purpose.

"You handle yourself well. I must admit to still being surprised an archivist has such grace with weapons."

Her lips purse, drawing my gaze. "And I still do not know why I let you leave unscathed yesterday."

"I gather you did not tell anyone about my visit either? Seeing as an army did not wait in ambush."

I am not paying much mind to the words coming out of my mouth. Instead, I enjoy the feast for the eyes she presents tonight. The oil lamps bathe her form in a warm orange light, casting her silhouette onto the wall behind her. I can feel my chest expanding with deeper breaths as my heart beats stronger, finally getting what it yearned for all day – the sight of its treasure.

35

Syrin fidgets under my scrutiny, no doubt feeling the intensity of my fascination with her. "I have thought of nothing else all day, demon."

The defensive tone of her voice brings a smile to my face and I turn to pry the knife free. Closing the distance between us, I purposefully make my gait predatory, pushing her boundaries. Let us see how long until she throws something at me again.

"I have thought of nothing but you all day as well, angel," I whisper, extending the knife to her, handle first and holding its bottom. The move pays off instantly as her fingers brush against mine. She freezes and I take advantage of that as well, caressing her pointer finger with my thumb. In response, her mouth opens on a gasp and I cannot help smirking.

"Why do you talk to me like that?" Her question is a whisper, and I move closer by instinct, as if our conversation is a secret no one may overhear. Which, I concede, it is.

"How? As if you are everything I ever think about anymore?"

Her throat bobs as she swallows. "Yes."

My smirk widens into a grin. "Because it is true."

Her eyes widen before she looks away from my face. First I think she is looking at our hands, still connected by her dagger. Then I notice she is watching my torso instead, the shirt I am wearing tight over my chest. Slowly, I lift my other hand to caress the exposed skin of her arms again.

"I swear I could feel you under my fingertips all day, *Gilsa*."

Syrin tears her eyes away from the muscles of my chest and they shimmer in the flickering light as they meet mine.

"Do you ever wonder what it would be like to feel more?" I ask quietly.

"More of what?" She sounds breathless, and the animal part of me enjoys exploiting her weaknesses.

Emboldened, I move my other hand higher, my fingers sliding over hers, over her wrist, and under her elbow until I hold both of her arms loosely. I want to pull her closer, but I know I must keep her far enough that she does not escape from the feelings our contact is

36

surely stirring within her. My eyes narrow on the sight of her parting lips and the little panting breaths escaping from between them.

"A demon should not be touching an angel this way."

Ignoring her whispered observation, I continue the sensual exploration of the object of my obsession. As I touch the sensitive flesh on the inside of her arms, she begins to tremble. Slowly, I glide my thumbs over the feather-soft skin, from the inner crook of her elbow to the tops of her shoulders. I can hear her heart beginning to race alarmingly and I stop in my tracks. Her breaths begin to audibly saw in and out and she leans in as if she cannot hold herself straight anymore. I bring my face in line with hers, then brace her arms with my hands.

"Syrin. Calm, *Muluskara.* It is just your body reacting to touch, you are in no danger."

She looks at me, her head shaking in denial. "I have never felt like this before. No one has touched me like that."

"I have never touched anyone like that either." Her face scrunches up in confusion. It is very amusing to see on such a dignified creature. She likely thinks I am lying to her. Is that not what demons do? Lie, bed anything remotely attractive, and kill the rest. I cannot resist caressing the sides of her arms with my thumbs. "I am not lying. Did you... find it pleasant?" I wait for her answer like a thief waits for a quorum to decide his fate. Will he keep his hands attached to his body?

She lowers her gaze. "I am unsure." Her full cheeks flush and the sight is nearly enough to bring an honest smile to my face. A part of what she said must be a lie that she feels guilt over.

"You should leave." Though her voice is uncertain, her words were not an invitation to explore these new and exciting sensations together – but I have no desire to leave now that I am finally in her presence again.

"I have dreamt of touching you every night since that day on the battlefield," I breathe. It is best if I do not share the expulsion of bodily fluids that always follows such dreams. Even a novice at seduction such as me knows that.

Her mouth opens, lips forming an 'o' of surprise. "Have you ever thought of me?" I push gently, moving my head an inch closer to hers.

Cheeks flushed anew, she stutters a few times. My lips begin to curl at the outer edges and just as I become certain she will let me stay tonight, the sound of light footsteps approaching reaches us from the outside.

We both turn our faces in the direction of her door. Not wasting a moment, I spin around in search of a hiding place. I do not think any angel here could best me in a fight, but I do not want to cause my treasure needless distress. The only viable option is a wardrobe. Using the heightened speed Father blessed me with, I find myself in the near darkness among her jasmine-scented robes.

The scent of jasmine only increases as I feel a breeze enter through the wardrobe's cracks. Syrin must have used the ether to call up scented winds from outside in order to mask my presence. I often wish Father had given me more powers over the fabric of the universe. He must have thought giving me advantages, such as calling hellfire or traveling great distances in the blink of an eye, would have made me a bigger threat than I am.

My eyes adapt to the dark until I see as clearly as I would in the mortals' daylight. I can hear a new female voice inquiring about the archive's tablets and my angel acquiescing to lend them to her, but my mind is focused only on what I see sticking out of the pocket of one of Syrin's robes. I reach until my hand is hovering over a dozen feathers of varying sizes, each white with a silvery-purple iridescence. Has she been collecting her fallen feathers? Why? My fascination is widely known, but most consider it grotesque, even a number of Hell's residents. Could she have truly been thinking of me? Carefully, I collect my prize.

I bring the largest to my nose to draw her scent into my lungs, and close my eyes in pleasure. Just as I cup and squeeze my now once again erect manhood, the wardrobe opens. Syrin gasps and I open my eyes to see one hand clutching the fabric of her nightdress above her breasts, the other slapped over her mouth. I need to leave before we wake every angel in the vicinity with the sounds I plan to extract from her in the near future.

I give her a salacious grin, then tuck my new treasure securely into the inside pocket of my cloak. "Thank you for this precious gift." I step out of the wardrobe and walk to the door, knowing well I am doing so with exaggerated swagger. Her eyes track me the entire way. "I will return tomorrow night," I promise.

She splays her fingers enough that she can speak through her hand. "You should not."

"But I will." With one last look at my angel, I ease the door open. Once I see the path of escape is clear, I join the shadows once more.

CHAPTER 5

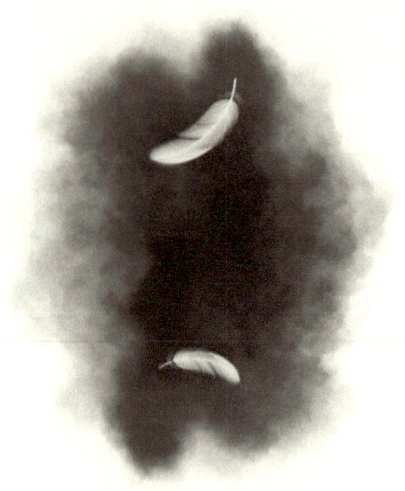

What is that?"

I have been visiting my angel nightly, and she has grown accustomed to my presence, at least enough that she no longer feels the need to keep a close eye on my every movement. Unfortunately, she had made no physical contact a condition for allowing my presence here. That did, however, leave hours upon hours of time to talk, leading to a different kind of intimacy. One that I did not expect to enjoy so much.

Earlier, Father asked to see me. While he said that he wished to know my opinion on the War's progression, I left his domain feeling disquieted. He wished to know where I have been spending my nights, making it obvious he had been observing me. I gave him excuses, but he always knows *everything*. I worry for my angel's safety, should he desire to teach me a lesson for whatever slight he perceives me to make.

"I have been attempting to expand the written Malachim language," Syrin answers, bringing my thoughts back to the present. "Humans have now started to write as well, and their methods are incredibly innovative. With how brief their lives are, it is no wonder how quickly they advance."

For a moment I enjoy observing her efforts in silence. Then curiosity wins. "What are you recording now?" I only have a view of the side of her face, but it is enough for me to see the telltale blush covering the curve of her cheek. I grin, something that hurt my cheeks at first, but the muscles grew as strong as the rest with practice. "Is it about me?"

She tucks an errant curl behind her ear, the movement of her elegant fingers charming me anew. "I am describing your feats in battle."

Her finding me worthy of recording caresses a slowly healing part of me, one that I never noticed before, but now know has always been painful. "You observed me?" My voice comes out huskier than usual and she throws me a quick glance before focusing on her runes.

"You were the most interesting part of the battle."

Thinking of her watching me as I heave and swing my sword, untouchable to my enemies, instantly makes my leathers too small around my pelvis. I took myself in hand before visiting her, as I have done every night, but it never seems to lessen the desire I feel for her. Surreptitiously, afraid she may deny me her companionship – the only friendship I have ever had – If I got caught, I shift in my seat, tugging on my trousers.

Judging by the way she freezes, my efforts at stealth were wasted. Her eyes meet mine and they seem to shimmer with awareness. Common sense leaving me again, I lean forward and whisper, "Have you ever caressed your body while thinking of me?"

Face engulfed in red, she shakes her head. "I told you, no touching."

"And I am not touching you. Incidentally, I never said you may not touch me. Feel free to do so any time the urge strikes." I place my hand atop her desk, dangerously close to hers. "I have," I answer my own question. "Every day, oftentimes several times a day."

She takes a quick glance at my hand's new location, then meets my eyes again in rapt attention. Titillated, I push further. "I attempted to touch myself elsewhere, but my callused hands could never trick my mind into believing they were yours. So I always just reach between my legs."

Eyes unwillingly drawn to my lap, she inhales sharply when she spots the large bulge at the center of it. Her small finger moves closer to mine infinitesimally, as if drawn there. "I take one of your feathers and bring it against my lips." Syrin's eyes are now locked onto my mouth. I roll my lips together and wet them with my tongue. I can hear her heart racing. "I squeeze my shaft, thinking of how incredible it would feel to have you there." As her gaze jumps back to my groin, I ask her quietly, "Do you wish to see it?"

I was certain she would say no, but her wild eyes settle on mine again, daring me to take her lack of denial as the answer I wish to hear. Growling lowly, I clumsily use my other hand to unclasp my leathers and pull them down enough to unleash my trapped cock. Her eyes are still on mine as I fist my pulsing member, lids shutting reflexively.

When I open them again, her chin is tipped down and shallow breaths leave her lips in tiny bursts of air. My Syrin's eyes are on my cock. I groan quietly as I squeeze the root harder, and the plum-shaped head turns darker from an abundance of trapped blood.

"Neph," she whispers, the diminutive warming my heart and sending a pulse of lust to my cock.

"Syrin," I reply just as quietly, beginning to shuttle my fist up and down the length of my manhood. "My Syrin."

Her hand moves, tentatively at first, just her pinky sliding over my fingers, then all of hers wrap around them, squeezing nearly as hard as I am squeezing myself. This will be over pathetically fast.

"I long to taste you on my tongue." Breaths rough, I hunch forward as pleasure twists in my stomach. Then I see my angel's thighs are pressed tightly together from my words, as if she hungers too. It is my undoing.

I groan long and deep as the tension of pleasure snaps, and the first stream of come shoots into the air before covering the fist still diligently milking out my orgasm. Seeing Syrin's hungry eyes and hearing the little breathless moan she cannot hold in at the sight of my release, makes my body whip back, moving the chair I sit on, as another pulse of semen erupts from my cock. "Syrin, Syrin, Syrin," I chant relentlessly over the increasingly louder sounds of wet flesh being manipulated.

Sighing as my body turns boneless, I ease the movements of the hand in my lap, and use the thumb of the one on the desk to caress Syrin's still tightly clenched fingers.

Any bliss I feel dissipates instantly as a knock sounds at the entrance of her home.

"Syriniana? Is everything alright? I heard a noise."

The male's voice raises every animal instinct in my body, urging me to protect my mate from encroaching suitors. My lips peel into a silent snarl.

My angel's eyes dart to the door. Releasing my hand, she takes a bracing inhale. "I am fine!" Her voice has a trembling quality, but she sounds a lot more chipper than she looks. "I was clumsy, I banged the chair!"

She just lied to, in her eyes, protect *me*. Or perhaps she lied to protect the male outside *from* me. Rage turns my vision red and Syrin squeezes my now-fisted hand again.

The male is silent for a moment, then finally replies, "I am unused to you being graceless." Just how well does he know her?

"Oh, I must be more tired than I thought! Good night!" Her lip is caught between her teeth again, as we wait to see whether the male will accept her explanation.

"All right. Good night."

His retreating steps quiet before Syrin speaks again. "You must leave now."

Wincing, I stuff my spent member into my trousers, then wipe my hand against them. "Allow me to take care of your need," I implore, thoughts now back to the way she clenched her thighs.

She was shaking her head before I even finished speaking. "No," she says. "We cannot. We should not have done this. I will fall!" Her voice is more urgent with every word, until the last is said with a hiss.

I flip our hands on top of the desk until I can squeeze her fingers. "And I will catch you," I vow.

She scoffs, but after a moment of hesitation, lifts our hands to her mouth to place a kiss atop mine. "Good night, Nephithar."

Sighing, I resign myself to the fact that this will go no further tonight.

"Good night, *Muluskara*."

CHAPTER 6

Battle erupts again the next day, and I find myself among an overwhelmingly large number of angels before I can obsess over the events of the previous night. It has been a while since Heaven sent such a host.

Ripping off my opponent's breastplate with brute force, I take a second to enjoy his expression of slack incredulity. With a chuckle, I rear back before thrusting my sword into his stomach with both hands. Slicing upwards until blade meets ribcage, I watch the silvery blood drip from his mouth with fascination. It is amazing how well a Celestial's mortal form mimics its namesake.

Growing tired of him quickly, I kick him off my weapon, causing a silver arc to form in the air before it showers me. The color reminds me of *my* angel and I feel a moment's bite of conscience before shaking it off. It would take a lot more than a little gutting to destroy an angelic warrior. Indeed, my former opponent disperses his humanoid shape before fully hitting the ground, floating off to safety.

It is a miracle no one on Hell's side noticed I have not slain a single angel in the last couple of weeks. I did not suddenly misplace my enjoyment of battle, no, I merely find the thought of spending the night with Syrin, knowing I had likely killed a friend of hers that day, distasteful.

In the split second of inattentiveness, another angel manages to charge me, hitting my side hard enough that I briefly fly through the air, before crashing onto the dusty, blood-sprayed ground. I roll to my feet with my sword already swinging, catching the warrior under the chin just as he leaps back, slicing into his once-flawless face.

Spitting out dust mixed with whatever moisture is left in my mouth, I begin to circle my newest opponent. He caught me off guard and deserves a longer fight than most. The angel sniffs, being able to do so only by the grace of two inches separating his nose from the gushing wound.

"Why do you smell of Syriniana?"

This sounds like the warrior who interrupted us yesterday. Suddenly, I no longer feel so magnanimous. Hearing her name uttered by another male is infuriating.

"Of whom?" I ask as I diminish the space between us and aim a backhanded sweep towards the side of his torso, surprising him enough that my sword cuts several inches deep, ruining the kidney he does not really require, but is a prerequisite of this form. He stumbles back, a hand pressed against what would be a fatal wound for a mortal.

"The female angel," he continues the conversation as if we were not in the middle of a duel. "Did you harm her?"

I feel relief for all of a second. He does not suspect her of meeting with me; he thinks we fought. That relief is squashed the instant I realize she is here on the battlefield. There are so many angels here today, the demons are even more bloodthirsty than usual. Despite her being older and evidently intelligent enough to keep herself alive through conflict, the overwhelming urge to find her and see with my own two eyes that she is safe overtakes my entire being.

Since the angel is not suspicious of her, I have no excuse to eliminate Syrin's friend. A pity. "I have killed no female angels today," I answer truthfully, then I parry his weak attempt to behead me, before kicking him to the ground. Straddling him with my knees digging into his stomach, one right into the side of the wound, I press his arms down above his head. The angel cries out in agony, his marred face twisting and now far less beautiful. I may not intend to kill him, but last night's interruption deserves to be punished.

Him being blinded by pain gives me the opportunity I need to unsheathe a shorter sword, which I use to cut his hands off, one at a time. The nosy angel's agonized howls soothe the beast inside me. I jump up, slicking my hair back with a blood-streaked hand, before leaning down to retrieve my discarded greatsword.

The angel must realize he is not far from catastrophic damage and, finally, releases his mortal body before whisking away. He will never know I had no intention of finishing him off, nor the reasons behind it. There are moments where I fear I have become a pathetic imitation of myself as I was before Syrin. But in so many ways I have never felt stronger than I do now.

Roaring with renewed vigor, I take on two angels at once, a male and female pair of gilded warriors. Falling into the intrinsic rhythm of strike and dodge, strike and parry, I find myself experiencing what could possibly be happiness for the first time. I will spend the day doing what I do best, bathing the battlefield in silvery blood, then once evening comes, I will spend the night doing what feels best – basking in my lilac moon's radiant glow. I feel like a dandelion puff floating in a gentle breeze – and I would cut my right arm off before saying that aloud.

Mortals have a redundant saying; something about counting one's poultry before it leaves its shell. At least, I always found it to be redundant, likely because I never had anything to look forward to beside battle. As Heaven's archangels descend from the orange sky, bathing the combat zone in white, I slowly lower my sword.

Before the last of them touches the ground, rumbling footsteps sound behind me. The ground shakes as I turn to see Azeal, the largest among Hell's royalty, enter the fray, a walking mountain. Asmodai, the youngest among Father's most trusted, saunters behind him, not a care on his face, only vague amusement.

Clearly he is not thinking what I am thinking; we are all about to die in a most permanent way. A clash between these giants will be ruinous.

"Brothers!" Belial's tone, full of false surprise, echoes through the plain, enhanced to be heard by all. "To what do we owe this delightful visit?"

Hell's army reacts with mirth, huffs of laughter rising up among the ranks. The archangels, however, remain as expressionless as always. While the angels around them sniffed in disgust – a considerably overt showing of emotion for them – the archangels themselves do not deign to acknowledge Belial's provocations.

"The War has gone on long enough, and we will allow no more casualties." Uriel, Heaven's wisest, steps to the front of what has become a clear delineation between the two opposing factions.

Asmodai snickers. "If *we* fight, everyone here will perish in moments." His head may be between some creature's legs the

49

majority of the time, but it seems to be one of the few ones thinking of consequences.

Uriel blatantly ignores him. I do not think it is because he disagrees with the observation, merely that he is so far beneath his notice; being born in Hell and so very much younger than others in power.

"This represents the final opportunity for us to engage in discussions regarding the potential for neutrality," Uriel says and, in reaction, Azeal hocks up before spitting on the ground.

"And what, exactly, did you have in mind to offer in return for us giving up unfettered access to our food source?" Belial's question is met with support from Hell's basest creatures, especially those that feed off flesh.

"As humanity finds itself increasingly subject to your influence—"

"We merely gave them free will," Asmodai mutters.

"The number of corrupted souls rises." Uriel continues as if never interrupted. "The most depraved among sinners shall be sent to your realm upon their demise, so that you may feed upon them in perpetuity."

I look around to check my comrades' reactions. I know many prefer a hands-on approach to feeding, but a steady stream of sinners' energies would solve many issues. Still, most seem skeptical. Malaphar is tossing an ether-summoned ball of hellfire in the air before catching it and starting anew, seemingly ready to select a target at a moment's notice.

"In order to safeguard humanity, in the interest of both sides, a council shall be convened, wherein each party shall hold an equal vote," Uriel finishes.

"What does that mean?" someone asks behind me.

"That is ridiculous!" exclaims another.

Before long, everyone is voicing their opinion regarding Heaven's proposition at once, giving me a headache more surely than when an angel banged his shield against my skull mere hours ago.

"He will discuss it."

Ashtaroth, who has always been my Father's favorite — a truth which caused me no small amount of envy — never speaks much, but when he does, everyone listens. Father must have been observing the interaction and spoke directly to him. To *him*, and not me, his son.

"There is a desert realm of no consequence by The Phlegethon. We volunteer it for the purpose of this neutral meeting... and any potential others in the future." Ashtaroth's words leave little in the way of ambiguity. Shouting erupts as the demons around us begin to realize there may be no more excursions to the human lands.

"Quiet!" I roar at them, my first words since the archangels descended. These demons, at least, still know I am their general and turn towards me. "Who are you to gripe over Father's wishes?"

Silence descends onto the field and I face the front again. While Uriel's expression remains the same, I can see traces of disgust in his brilliant eyes. It appears that someone just realized who I am; Angelbane, The Butcher of Hell, the Spawn of Satan. I sneer and give him a mocking bow.

If these negotiations bear fruit, will there still be any reason for Syrin to visit Hell? They do not consider me an 'archdemon', but as the creation Sataniel calls son, will I be confined to Hell as well?

I hide the storm raging within by glowering at anyone who dares make eye contact. I must get to my angel as soon as possible.

CHAPTER 7

Tonight, while the angels are all grounded and talking about the battle, the best way to traverse their camp unseen is by moving above the winged creatures.

Descending from Syrin's roof as soundlessly as possible, I enter her home with the speed born from several consecutive days of practice. This is the first time I find myself alone in it. She must not be back yet or is, perhaps, conversing with the others, taking notes of the battle from different perspectives.

Restless, I pace the one-room home. My eyes take in items with which she has likely been passing time lately; pottery, baskets, even small carpets, though I do not see a loom. Every item is perfect to me, especially the vase with the tiny nick near the bottom.

How do I convince her not to leave me behind, as surely as the warriors here will leave Hell behind if a truce is achieved? How does one convince someone who has everything they need to forsake it all for a flawed and corrupted creation?

The sound of soft steps outside signals her arrival. Her silvery brows hike up when she sees me standing in the middle of her home. As soon as the door is shut behind her, I reach for my angel and pull her into my arms. It is immediately painfully obvious neither of us has ever participated in an embrace. She stands stiffly, unable to move her arms as they are pinned to the sides.

I lean back slightly, my words rushing out. "Forgive me," I begin, still holding her at arm's length. "I only breached your rule against physical contact because I am immensely relieved to see you unharmed after today."

She smiles at me tentatively, both of us clearly aware that I have yet to remove my hands from her arms, but not speaking on it. "I am well, Neph."

Every time she calls me by my name, especially in the shortened form only she has ever used, I feel a flutter in my chest, as if I could fly even without wings. "I would like to take you somewhere," I declare.

She tilts her head. "Where?"

"Allow me some mystery," I tease her.

I could live off her warm smiles, every rare one she would decide to grace me with. I release a breath at her acceptance, only now realizing a part of me feared that she would not trust me with herself outside of this cottage.

I let my hands slide down her arms until they reach hers, taking hold of her fingers in a similar fashion to last night's, but with a vastly different emotion behind the action. "Meet me outside the eastern edge," I whisper. Moving around her, I exit her home as carefully as always – now is not the moment to get caught. Not when this may be the last time I use this door.

Shimmying up the trellises, I silently apologize for trampling her jasmine, just beginning to bloom as night is setting in. Crossing her roof, I make sure no one is in the narrow alleyway before jumping over to the next. I repeat the process until I reach my usual point of entry, then skirt the walls until the eastern part of them is in sight. Syrin stands there, Hell's replica of the Moon, with her wings now out.

This is the first time I lay eyes upon them again since that first day and find myself just as mesmerized as I was then. I imitate a warbler's mating call to draw her attention. She shakes her head at the sound, but follows it into the greenery, her wings more beautiful the closer they get.

"When was the last time you heard a songbird in Hell?" Her words have a teasing edge, immediately making this the most enjoyable conversation I have ever had. Well, if one does not count her whispering my name as she watched me bring myself to orgasm.

Fidgeting to dispel the memory, I return her teasing. "When I first visited you and you were humming while weaving."

Looking away as if to hide the flush on her cheeks, she does not hesitate with a riposte. "Is visiting what you call invading someone's home uninvited?"

"Your door was unbarred, clearly I was invited."

Her chuff warms my heart and I reach out for her hand. Damn the no-touching rule tonight. "None of us lock our doors."

54

"Well," I say, addressing her wings, as I cannot seem to take my eyes off them. "It is a good thing then, that only you know a monster may come in."

"Ah, a monster." A corner of her mouth lifts. "I hear there were no casualties again this battle."

"Shush, if this becomes known, then more females will attempt to tame their monsters. There will be no worthy villains left in the world."

"Why yes," she chuckles. "The story of our friendship will be passed down for generations."

"Eons," I breathe, feeling as if the ground is shaking under me. My angel had claimed me as a friend.

"You..." She trails off and I move my eyes to her face. She is biting her lower lip again. "You could touch them if you wanted to."

"Your wings?" Taken aback, I can feel my jaw go slack. Why would she let me, of all creatures, touch her delicate wings?

Syrin takes a bracing inhale. "Yes."

I hesitate for a moment, still in disbelief, and observe her face for any signs that she may not mean it, or may have changed her mind since uttering the words, a mistake. When her eyes bravely hold mine, my chest tightens with joy. I reach a reverent hand towards the leading edge of her left wing, the very one that was injured that day. First, I softly trail just the tips of my fingers over it.

She inhales a ragged breath and my eyes snap back to her face immediately. Once she nods with a shaky smile, I take a step closer and return to my exploration, my knuckles following the length of the underwing as I reach down in the direction of the tip. Once I reach as far as I can while remaining standing, I extend my fingers and roll them over the edge until they gently brush through the longer feathers of the trailing edge. Touching an uninjured wing, *her* wing, going as slow as I wish... this has to be the topmost sensory experience of my life.

The changing cadence of her breath stirs me an immeasurable amount more than the moans of any succubus ever could, and I can feel my leathers becoming tight. I stop before I turn into a beast while barely out of sight of the wall.

Taking a step back, I clear my throat. "Thank you." My words still come out rough, so I force a smile. Were I to live until the end of time, I would still not forget this moment.

I take a deep breath in an attempt to center myself, then bow, sweeping my arms and gesturing for her to precede me. "If you would head this way." Her round eyes, gray with a hint of lavender, sparkle, and I cannot tell whether it is with mischief or in an attempt to hide sadness.

We exchange few words until we reach the edge of a canyon. Below it, Lethe churns over rocks and descends in frothy rapids.

"There is a cave directly underneath us. The entrance is carved into the cliff face. We could climb down, or you could fly us."

Syrin tilts her head with a smirk. "Was this all a clever ploy to have me carry you through the air?"

I gently prod her in the ribs with a single finger. Now that I have given myself permission to touch her, I cannot seem to stop. "Naturally. I have been flown before, but, and you can trust me on this, flying with Hell's minions is in no way a pleasant ride."

She purses her lips. "I can imagine. Well, I have obviously never had to fly anyone before, so I cannot guarantee your enjoyment of the experience."

"Oh, trust me." I step closer and herd her towards the edge, until I can see the restless river over her shoulders. "I am bound to enjoy this immensely."

Her gaze flicks upward to meet mine and she swallows. "I would suspect your plan is to push me off a cliff, but that would be utterly pointless."

"I am disappointed you would consider suspecting *that* instead of me simply wanting your arms around me." My retort holds no venom, for we both know she is merely giving herself time to dispel her nerves.

Once she is ready, she opens her arms and I step into them. My chest presses against her breasts as we wrap our arms around each

56

other, and I close my eyes. I can feel her heartbeat, its tempo that of a gazelle futilely running from a lion. I go with her as she takes that final step back, wings fanning out to catch the air. Our weight tugs us towards the ground for the briefest of seconds, before she harnesses the current and gently steers us to the cave opening hidden by moss and vines.

"I never noticed this one."

"It is smaller and out of sight. With more obvious and easier options, few go looking for it."

"How did you find it then?"

I grin into her neck and she shudders at the feel of it. "I fell into it."

"You fell over the cliff edge? How?"

As she sounds positively aghast, I am able to hold onto a smile through the normally enraging memory. "I was pushed."

We touch down at the cave mouth and she leans back to gauge my expression. "Who could have pushed you?"

I can feel my smile turning brittle, so I give her a gentle squeeze before turning away. "That is a story for another day."

The word *never* hangs in the air as I use an arm to clear the path for her.

As soon as she passes by, I realize she had to dismiss her physical wings in order to fit into the narrow opening. A hollowness spreads inside my chest at the thought that I may never see them again, and I allow myself to wallow in it for a moment until her gasp brings me back to the present.

"Cave springs?"

At the sound of her elation, my chest feels somewhat lighter. "The water does wonders for sore muscles and bruises."

I unclasp my cloak, allowing it to pool on the ground, and start removing my leathers before she manages to sputter out words.

"What are you doing?"

"The pools ruin leather armor, I know this from experience." I wink at her as I remove my boots, delighting in the way she clutches her hands at her chest. With one final look at her stunned form, I turn towards the springs, drop my leathers and step out before wading into the water. Once it begins lapping around my chest, I let my body sink, enjoying the weightlessness.

I hear the muffled sounds of her approach and push up, slicking back my hair. She kneels by the pool's edge, eyes still comically wide. "I was worried for a moment."

"Syrin... You do realize breathing is somewhat optional for us?"

She flushes and looks at her reflection in the rippling water. "No one is sure of how you were created."

I lift my brows. "Ah." If I were an archivist, I would have asked about such physical characteristics as soon as we established a rapport. "Well, physically I am closer to humans than I am to angels, in the sense that I do not have an ethereal form, but eating, sleeping and breathing are still more of a suggestion than a requirement. I can go long without them unless I exert myself or am injured in battle."

"I see." She is looking anywhere but at me. "And were you made fully grown or as a child?"

I grin before pulling myself onto a ledge and leaning back, most of my torso now visible. I twine my fingers over my groin before answering her. "If you wish to know more about me, you will have to join me." Her eyes jump to my face, then my covered pelvis, before she flushes and takes a look at her robes. "Leave them on, if it makes you more comfortable, though I suggest you at least remove the cloak."

Fiddling with the ties, she takes my advice to remove her cloak, but then merely fidgets in place, wringing her hands. I pretend to be engrossed with the way water ripples in concentric circles from a tap of my fingertips, letting her gather the courage at her own pace. It helps to think of all the new things I have discovered since we met, reminding myself that most of our interactions are foreign and even forbidden to her. Gulping, my stomach warms as I realize just how much she has conceded already.

The swishing sound of clothing draws my gaze and my jaw goes slack at the sight before me. While I was lost in thought, she had stripped down to a simple sheath, like the one she wore the first time

58

I came to her home. Clenching and unclenching her fists a few times, she finally descends into the warm waters.

I watch as the silken white fabric turns darker at the contact with water, the hue climbing up as it saturates the material above the water's edge. She does not submerge into the water as I did, but instead timidly draws nearer. As she lifts her head, her eyes lock on mine. I feel like a sailor ensnared by a siren, yet instead of raw sexuality being her weapon, she has enchanted me with her pureness and innocence.

"My Syrin," I murmur as the tips of my angel's silver hair meet the water and begin to float gently around her. The steam starts to carry the scent of jasmine and I inhale deeply. "You are the most exquisite creature in the cosmos."

She dips her head and, with her robes out of the way, I can now see the flush from her cheeks also suffusing her décolletage. She joins me on the ledge but leaves a distance between us. I fight the urge to reassure myself that she is still close enough to touch. "So," she prompts.

"So. I was formed as you see me now." I would not dream of denying her the answer after she so bravely acquiesced to my demand. Her gaze sweeps over my naked form, hardly covered by the shallow water, my manhood shielded only by my tented hands. Her eyes linger there and she wets her lips.

No longer fighting the urge to do what I have been dreaming of every time we met at night, I slowly turn until I am on all fours and begin to crawl towards my angel. Her eyes follow every shift of bare muscle. Once I draw close enough, I sit back on my haunches and reach for her mouth. Using my thumb, I gently pry the abused lip free.

"Have you ever been kissed?" I ask, just as I did on a night not long ago, knowing well the answer. My question is a statement of intent.

"We should not be doing this," she breathes, her brows drawn as if she is in pain.

"I will not allow this to be the last time I see you, *Muluskara*, but if I were to perish in battle tomorrow without having kissed you… then it was not a life worth living."

A warm, trembling exhale caresses the thumb still resting on her chin, before she dips her head in surrender.

"Show me. Show me what it is like to feel."

CHAPTER 8

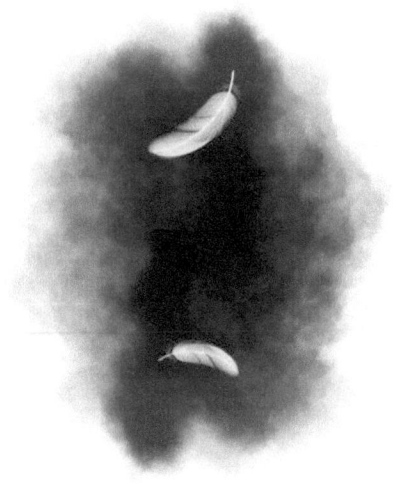

My world narrows down to the scent of jasmine and the color silver. To the satin touch of her skin against my fingertips as I guide her mouth towards mine. Leaning in, I join our lips in the gentlest of pressures. Her shiver prompts me to place my hands on her arms, an innate response to soothe and protect.

Tilting my head, I press firmer and use my lips to open hers wider. My nose meets her warm cheek just as I feel the featherlight touch of her hand at the small of my back. "Yes," I whisper an encouragement into her mouth, and her fingers clench reflexively, urging me closer.

I allow my tongue to sweep inquisitively over her parted teeth until it meets the tip of hers with an electrifying jolt. Briefly losing touch with sanity and restraint, I slide my hands under her arms and pull her atop me, sealing my mouth to hers.

She pulls back, breathing heavily and my eyes open in alarm, fearing I had pushed her too far. Her eyes are wide with wonder and desire. I run a soothing hand down her back, then notice her legs are tangled in the heavy wet material. My hands move slowly, as if I am faced with a frightened doe, and I pick up the waterlogged hem. Checking her face for a reaction, I lift it until her knees can fall open to frame my legs. Moving her with my hands on her waist, I help her settle comfortably on my thighs. Though I am hard as a rock, something she would certainly notice were she to look down, I fight to keep my breathing even and my brow smooth.

"I cannot do this," she whispers, but belies the statement immediately by pressing her lips against mine again and giving me a glimpse of Heaven. The kiss is longer, our breaths mingling, hands cautiously exploring the other's body. I touch her reverently, an unparalleled feeling of possession warming my insides. I revel in the way she trembles, the way her breathing becomes audible with little sounds of need.

When she begins to squirm, I blindly lift the hem of her sheath to her waist and press our pelvises together with one quick pull. Her spine straightens in shock as she gasps my name. "I cannot go back if we do this," she pleads. "I will become an apostate; I will be alone."

I shake my head in vehement denial. "You will never be alone as long as I exist." I am not the same creature I was before I set eyes on her, and if she accepts my past, accepts who I am, then I will gladly spend eternity giving her whatever she needs.

With a sob, she once again melts into my embrace. I move my mouth to her neck and nuzzle it, pressing my lips against where I can most feel the rapid beating of her heart. My hands move to her breasts of their own volition, and my cock twitches against her core when I feel the firm peaks. Lost to lust, I rip her underclothing to the waist, bearing the twin mounds to my gaze for the first time.

Growling and overcome with greed, I try to take as much as I can into my mouth, before alternatively pulling on the tip and massaging it with my tongue. She tries to wiggle away from the sensations, so I hold her against me more firmly, pulling her down against me as I buck up. "Take what you need," I command.

"I do not know how," her trembling voice reaches my ear from where she rests her head atop mine. I lick a path from one breast to the other, ready to give it the same treatment. "There is such pressure."

I take a deep, grounding breath before I end up spilling against her soft center too soon. What have I done to deserve being the male who guides this magnificent creature to her pleasure? "Use my body," I all but growl against her sternum. Grabbing hold of the round flesh of her posterior, I urge her to grind her slick folds against my hardness. "Like that," I moan, sounding pathetic to my own ears, but she must not notice. Each time the hot flesh between her legs meets mine, she makes a sound that must have been created to loosen the dwindling hold I have over my sanity.

Attempting to speak over the lump in my throat — which I am convinced is my heart — I spur her on. "Does that feel good, Syrin?" When her only reply is a choked gasp, I squeeze her tighter. "Answer me," I order before finally taking the peak of her neglected breast in my mouth and pulling hard.

"Yes!" she moans loudly. I hope no angels are patrolling the length of the river today.

64

"What are you feeling?" I ask, greedy to know more.

"It is as if-" she breaks off on a gasp as I bite down on her nipple as gently as I can. "As if I burn," she says on an exhale, and I let the peak go.

It does not take long before any control I had evaporates and I start helping her ride me faster. Her cries turn almost painful as her limbs twitch intermittently. Every muscle in my body is on fire from lust. I fear that if I do not climax right now, my head will explode. "Let the pleasure take you," I plead. I pull back until I can look up at her face again. Silver hair frames her flushed face and her eyes shine with a lover's type of madness. "Let go for me."

Her eyes widen in surprise a moment before her head snaps back and she yells my name. Shouting in relief, I let myself follow, my cock pulsing and twitching against her softness, incredible slickness now easing the friction between our sexes. Clutching at her like a starving man clutches his last hunk of bread, I revel in the feeling of our hearts slowing in tandem, pressed close to each other.

A teardrop splashes against my shoulder and I hug my angel tighter. "Are you well?"

She clears her throat before answering. "Yes. Was that love?"

I shake with the attempt to hold my laughter in. "Yes. However, I think lust had a hand there, too."

Tenderly, I scoop her up and carry her to where our cloaks are pooled on dry ground, so that I can safely lay her on her back. I settle atop her, braced on my elbows. Her expression is the softest I have ever seen. I have yearned to have her gaze at me with such warmth and affection.

"Shall I make love to you now?" I ask, resting my forehead on hers, our noses kissing.

"Yes, please," she whispers against my mouth.

Taking that as a command, I reach between our bodies to caress her center, then enter her with one slickened finger. She gazes at me unflinchingly and with such trust, as if my hands have not been soiled by centuries of war. "Is this all right?"

She nods, making our noses slide against each other, before wrapping her arms around my neck. I hike up her thigh to give myself room and fist my still-hard cock.

I pause. "Are you certain?"

"You will catch me?"

I swallow in an attempt to ease the tightness in my throat and vow, my voice as hoarse as if I have been screaming commands in a week-long battle: "Every single time."

LIANA VALERIAN

CHAPTER 9

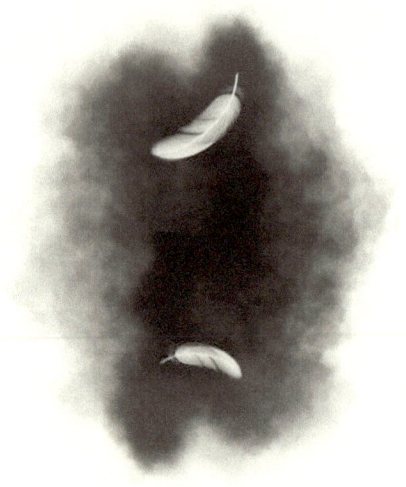

After making love – twice – and demonstrating what a determined male can achieve with his mouth, we lie in a heap, our hands still idly exploring every inch of skin within reach.

"Do you wish to live here, in this cave?" I do not need to voice the fact that Heaven is forever out of reach for her now, and soon, perhaps, even the mortal realm. I will furnish our new home lavishly, until it befits a queen.

She nods, rolling her lips together as she ponders. "Could you bring some things from my house? I do not think it wise to risk returning myself."

"Of course," I kiss the tip of her nose. Attempting to dispel the sadness from her eyes, I puff up my chest. "If it is your desire, I will rip the cottage from the ground and carry it to the cliff edge above us."

Her laughter does wonders to soothe the guilt I am unused to feeling. I drink in the sight of her smile until a foreign awareness freezes me. Terror such as I have never known sweeps through my body, raising every hair until even my scalp hurts.

"What is it?" Syrin asks. At the same time another voice sounds in my head, as familiar but utterly unwelcome.

"Son."

I clutch Syrin to me, wishing I could bury her inside my own body to keep her safe from the one who created me.

"Yes, Father?" I finally ask, knowing well we cannot hide from him in Hell.

"Take your angel and leave Hell immediately. You do not have much time."

My brows hike up in surprise. Syrin watches me with curiosity, clearly sensing a conversation she cannot hear is being had. *"Even if you do not hunt us, they will,"* I boldly challenge my sire.

For a moment there is no reply, but I can sense he has not left yet. Finally, he answers: *"As far as anyone is concerned, you both perished in battle today. Go live among the humans."*

I cannot believe what I am hearing. *"Why would you do this for me?"* My father has never treated me with any affection, and I have always known I am just a tool to him.

This time it takes even longer before his brusque voice returns. *"I do not need you anymore. The battles are over. You are useless to me now."*

With that, his presence disappears and I can once again focus on Syrin. Gaze patient, she waits for me to speak. I exhale slowly in an attempt to find my footing again after Father so unexpectedly tipped the foundations of my world, so leisurely changing the course of my entire existence.

"We are being allowed to leave Hell together, however, we must leave now." Though her brows inch together in a clear show of astonishment, she does not question the veracity of my claim. "Can you use the ether to travel?" I ask her.

She bites her lip and this time I let her. I regret that we do not have time for another round of lovemaking. "I can, but I am not yet strong enough to carry someone with me." It can take a few thousand years for angels to master the ether enough to move themselves freely through space and realms, and even longer for them to be able to take someone with them.

"No matter," I declare and jump to my feet. "Leave now and I will join you once I pass The Gates of Hell. Wait for me at Gehenna."

Her voice stops me while I am in the middle of threading one leg through my leathers. "No." She finds her sheath and pulls it on, tying the torn neckline into a knot. "I will not leave you. If anything slows you down and we get separated... I do not care where we live, even if it means losing my wings, as long as we are together."

Clumsily, I try to get both legs in my trousers, my skin dewy from the steam and hindering my success. Once my ass is covered, I reach for my angel and pull her into my arms.

"All right." I take a deep breath. "Together," I murmur into her sweet-smelling silver hair, then pull back and catch her gaze so I can give her a teasing wink. "Now, use those beautiful wings to carry your young love out of Hell."

70

*Keep reading for a preview of book one in The
Rivers of Hell – The River of Fire!*

THE RIVER OF FIRE

PROLOGUE – ASHTAROTH

We have discussed this several times, Belial." If the disinterested tone of my voice does not convey my boredom, the way I lounge in my seat, head resting on a fist, surely must. The archdemon in question faces me and his expression becomes pinched, lips thinned. While we have had no major conflicts these last millennia, Belial is well aware that the pool which is my tolerance is shallow indeed. His ingratiating manner depletes it quickly.

Belial lifts his arms in question, an ancient dramatic peacock. "I have been warning this Council for decades. What has to happen for us to act? A total loss of control over the human realm?" He tilts his head as if waiting for me to dig myself into a hole. Imbecile.

I release my breath in a sigh, lifting my head to have a better view of my fellow councilors. We meet on neutral ground, a cavernous space deep in the mountains of Purgatory. Naturally, Heaven and Hell are seated on opposing sides of the underground amphitheater-like structure. Only a few on the demonic side show some interest in Belial's plight. Asmodai winks at me, eyes twinkling. I look at Heaven's delegation next. Angels are harder to read, their expressions perpetually blank, but I imagine the news of manifested damned souls killing humans vexes them somewhat.

"What is Hell doing to prevent rifts remaining open between Hell and the human lands? If there are no rifts, there are no avenues for damned souls to escape through." The archangel Saraqael's powerful voice rumbles through the cavern. A contemporary of mine, Saraqael has a legendary stick up his tightly clenched asshole.

Belial shakes his head and the blonde ringlets of his mortal form bounce like released jack-in-the-boxes. "We all know rifts are notoriously hard to find. That isn't the solution here. We need to diminish the number of these manifestations so Hell isn't bursting at the seams."

Asmodai snorts, drawing all our gazes. "Perhaps we should implore the Transcendent and our Lord and Savior to finally increase the size of Hell? It's been the same size since humans plowed their first fields." My adopted brother's lips stretch into a wicked grin. "And we plowed our first humans."

Predictably, laughter erupts on our side and even I crack a smile. I have always preferred not to dally with humans, even before I was confined in the Underworld. They are too... fragile.

The other side, however, is less amused.

"Blasphemy!"

I am not certain which angel made their displeasure known as the outcry only fueled the demons' hilarity.

"Be quiet!" Belial's anger at our insouciance shows in the way he loses control over his form. Horns now poke out of the mop of angelic curls and his eyes are no longer cornflower blue, but instead glow a fiery orange. He never was very contained, though he tries hard to hide his demonic traits from the angels. "This is no time for jokes. If humans witness escaped denizens of Hell, they will destroy each other in the resulting chaos. Do you want to experience starvation, Asmodai?"

While Belial does have a flair for the dramatic, he is not lying. The majority of us seated on this side of the demarcation between Heaven and Hell once gained nourishment from Elysium. No longer welcome to partake there, we now feed on the power generated by sins. Humans, now numerous enough that the shedding of their mortal forms chokes Hell with overpopulation, are also its best source of food.

I lift my chin at Belial, resuming the pertinent conversation. "You wish to bring half-mortal offspring to Hell to assist with the numbers? They would be eaten within hours."

"Not Hell." Belial points at the ceiling.

"Purgatory?" Saraqael sounds almost intrigued. As intrigued as an emotionless mannequin can be.

"The Fallen of Abaddon have been culling the numbers alone for decades now. They would welcome assistance."

"That's debatable," Asmodai murmurs then raises his voice enough to be heard throughout the amphitheater. "Who would train them? The Elioud in the human realm are as powerless as any other mortal. Heaven made sure of that."

"Maalik of the Fallen spent time in my army. He is a capable warrior and leader. Since the offspring of Celestials aren't welcome in Heaven, Purgatory is as close to a neutral party in the Underworld as we can conceive of."

Belial's reply is quick and succinct. It is almost as if he had the answer ready, like a loaded cannonball waiting to be unleashed. He has been prattling about the dangers of Hell's overpopulation for years now, but it is obvious he had every step of what he sees as a solution planned.

"How many would you bring?" The angel inquiring is young – too young for me to have known him in Heaven and too insignificant to have bothered to learn his name since.

Belial still has munitions at the ready. "There are a few dozen physically appropriate Elioud with very few social attachments alive now."

The angel ponders for a moment. "And how will taking dozens of mortals risk exposure less than these sporadic attacks from Hell?"

"There are enough fallen angels in Abaddon to observe the suitable Elioud, then prepare and execute a simultaneous, stealthy extraction."

I scoff, making the archdemon turn towards me, jaw tight.

"And you think these mortals will want to help after being abducted into Hell?"

"Ashtaroth is correct, Belial." Saraqael shakes his head. "They may not have many attachments in the human realm, but their lives there are surely preferable to venturing into Hell, culling the ranks of mortal souls given form, and any ravenous demonic minions they meet while doing so."

Belial's expression turns bashful and I wonder if I am the only one who is repulsed by his artificial countenance. We did not rebel all those eons ago to pretend we are something we are not when Heaven observes.

"Unfortunately, they won't have a choice. We'll have to impart the importance of their mission. Make them see it as their purpose."

The air buzzes with noise as the assembled members each start voicing their conflicting opinions, but my attention is on Asmodai, who leans in with a mischievous smirk. "Mortals in Hell. It's been so long since I got to play with any." He pouts, and though he is thousands of years old, he now looks like the young Celestial I took under my wing when Lilith and Samael proved to have not a single parental bone between them. "No one summons me out of here anymore."

I huff and raise my brows in warning. "Be careful. Your cock gets you in trouble enough without mortals loose in Hell."

My brother waves a hand in dismissal. "Eh. What's Heaven going to do to me if I stoke a couple of Elioud's lust?"

I shake my head and focus on the discussion again. It looks like Belial will finally fulfill his desire to be the initiator of a momentous decision within the Council.

ACKNOWLEDGMENTS

December 2024

This novella wouldn't be here if it weren't for S.L., the original cheerleader, alpha reader, and editor. ♥

Maïté, thank you for alpha reading, and Poppy, for alpha reading, line editing, and abhorring anachronisms. ♡

My beta readers, notably Sharon, Ebony, and Ivy, also helped to improve The Gates of Hell for your reading pleasure. ♥

A round of applause for my Minion Amy, who created the wonderful map we can use as a reference. Another for Shaunie who created this gorgeous cover. ♡

A huge thank you to the rest of my Dream Team, Minions, and ARC readers as well for the incredibly lovely feedback, social media (and emotional) support, and general badassery. ♥

Lisa K. Byus for helping me with ancient Sumerian and Akkadian. ♡

Nowhere Eternity for letting our readers hear Neph's voice in snippets. ♥

Last but not least, thank you to whoever is still reading this (you completionist, you) – your support means the world and I'm eternally grateful. ♡

ABOUT THE AUTHOR

LIANA VALERIAN

Liana Valerian is a passionate gamer, obsessed bookworm, enthusiastic sci-fi and fantasy nerd, and self-proclaimed crazy cat lady. She crafts dark fantasy romance novels filled with humor, spice, and mythology, blending gothic and romantic elements in shadowy realms where darkness reigns.

Liana's debut novel, The River of Fire, the first in The Rivers of Hell series, is a steamy romance set in the Underworld, where angels, demons, and forbidden love collide.

You can follow her adventures and connect with her on social media @liana.valerian.

Title: The Gates of Hell
Subtitle: The Rivers of Hell 0.5
Author: Liana Valerian
ISBN 978-961-07-2424-7
Alternate cover edition
Self-published by Liana Valerian, Brežice, 2024
Print on Demand
Cover art and design by Shaunie Anne Schoonejans
Editing by MK Stephenson